THE PLAN

by Sharon Fear
illustrated by Phillip Dvorak

Scott Foresman

Editorial Offices: Glenview, Illinois • New York, New York
Sales Offices: Reading, Massachusetts • Duluth, Georgia
Glenview, Illinois • Carrollton, Texas • Menlo Park, California

Tap. Tap. Tap.
Was there a thing in the apartment?

"Come on, dog," said Jack.
"Now sleep close to me."

Tick. Tick. Tick.
Was there a BIG thing in
the apartment?
Could it be an elephant?

"Come on, cat," said Jack.
"Now sleep close to me."

Bump. Ping! Plink!
"That is too much!" said Jack.
"Now it sounds like pianos playing.
Dog, cat, I have a plan."

"MEOW!" yelled the cat.
"RUFF! RUFF!" yelled the dog.
"BE QUIET! NOW YOU NEED
TO GO TO SLEEP!" yelled Jack.
"That is the plan."

And that is what they did.